*DEAR SANTA is a Christmas tale for all ages that will be a holiday tradition for generations to come. Year after year, this cherished book will come to life, filling your home with the true spirit of Christmas... that sharing what is within, is the greatest gift of all.*

We wish to acknowledge the work of UNICEF on behalf of all the children of the world.

United States Committee for

**unicef**

United Nations Children's Fund

# Dear Santa

Adapted by Patrick S. Kleinen
from the original story by Michael Twinn

Illustrated by Patricia D. Ludlow

This edition published exclusively for
**Discovery Toys, Inc.** by
Child's Play (International) Ltd.

The tiny citizens of Santa's Village were filled with excitement.
It was the day before Christmas and Santa Claus,
who had been away a long time, was on his way home.
When Santa's sleigh appeared in the sky, they
cheered and waved and danced around.

"Ho! Ho! Ho! Hello! Hello, my special friends!" Santa
laughed and spread his big arms to hug them all at once.
"It is good to be home! What a wonderful year I have had!"
said Santa Claus. "And how are all of you? Are we ready
for Christmas?"

G. Willikers stepped forward. As Santa's First Helper, he was in charge of making all the preparations for Santa's Christmas ride.

"Everything is ship-shape, Santa Claus!" said Willikers.
"Come and see the Toyhouse. It's absolutely filled with wonderful toys for all the girls and boys!"

"I'm very impressed, Willikers!" Santa said as he looked at all the toys. "I see you have been very busy."

"We've made every kind of toy imaginable, Santa Claus."

"Yes indeed! But can you possibly get all of this packed into the sleigh before I leave tonight?"

Willikers smiled and shrugged his shoulders.
"I sure hope so, Santa!  The children are counting on us!"

Santa Claus and Willikers went up to the office where
Gumdrop and the others were sorting Santa's letters.

"The children sure write a lot of letters, don't they
Gumdrop?" asked Santa with a chuckle and a smile.

"Oh, yes, Santa Claus," she said, "and each one is so
sweet…but there are so many!  We need a computer just to
sort them all.  How in the world do you keep track of all
the boys and girls, Santa?"

"It's easy," he said with a gentle smile, "I simply love each child for who they are. And since no two people are the same, I never get confused. Do you understand?"

"I think so," Gumdrop giggled.

Santa laughed his wonderful laugh.

Santa Claus picked up a letter. It was from Teddy.

*Dear Santa,*

*I can't wait for Christmas. We're having a party on Christmas Eve and all my friends will come over. That's my favorite part of Christmas. But my other favorite part is PRESENTS! Can you bring me a globe? I want to know more about the world. I also want a basketball because I'd like to be a star player someday.*

*Love,*

*Teddy*

Santa smiled a long time. He loved Teddy and was glad that Teddy was such a happy boy. Santa would be sure to bring him a beautiful globe.

Santa Claus closed his eyes to think awhile. He thought about his friends, Janna and Thomas, whom he saw last week. "Little Janna and Thomas vowed to wait up all night to see me come down the chimney!" Santa said to himself, "I won't be surprised to find them fast asleep by the fireplace! Ho! Ho! Ho!"

Santa laughed quietly and drifted off to sleep.

Suddenly, Willikers came running in.
"Santa Claus! Wake up, Santa Claus!
Gumdrop just showed me the most
wonderful letter. It's from Kayla!"

Santa was happy to see Kayla's letter.
"She's such a caring little girl," he said.

Dear Santa,

Shawn and David and Vivian and I can't wait to see what you bring us this year...but we want you to know that it's okay if you don't bring us anything. We have a lot already. So if you run out of presents, make sure you take care of other kids who don't have as much as we do. But I do have a question for you. What do you do the rest of the year? I told Mom it's always Christmas wherever you go. Is that true?

Merry Christmas, Santa Claus!

Love,

Kayla

P.S. I really really want a pair of pink mittens with little flowers on top!

"I declare, Willikers, I wish everyone were as generous as my friend Kayla."

Santa felt very proud of Kayla.

"Willikers," Santa said through his big, white beard, "please make sure all the children's toys are packed in the sleigh. I'll be right down after I write a little letter to Kayla."

*Dear Kayla,*

*Merry Christmas, my special friend! Thank you for your thoughtful letter. It's my favorite one this year! Ho! Ho! Ho!*

*You are absolutely right! When it's not Christmas, my reindeer and I fly around the world bringing special gifts to people in need. And wherever I go, I take Christmas with me. I believe that Christmas is about caring for others and bringing joy to everyone we meet. So I treat every day like Christmas Day!*

# Santa's letter continued.

*Just yesterday I visited a school where the children had no books to read. I brought one for every boy and girl. And I read them a story, too!*

*In some places the children don't have medicine.*
*So my helpers and I bring it to them.  All children are precious to me.*
*And if they are sick, I do everything I can to make them feel better.*

Other children live where there is very little water.
So we help the people dig wells to make sure no one is thirsty.
It's hard work, Kayla! Sometimes I wish I were young like you!
Ho! Ho! Ho!

*It makes me sad, Kayla, but some people live where there is war.*
*No one likes war, especially children, so I bring peace with me when I visit.*
*I try to help people see how, working together, we can make this a better world…*
*for everyone.*

*I visit the animals, too! Last month I asked the elephants what I could do to help them. They said, "Santa, help us protect our habitat!" I said, "What a wonderful idea!" So I work to keep the wilderness wild and the animals free. It's a busy life being Santa Claus! Ho! Ho! Ho! I need all the help I can get. I'm counting on you and Vivian and David and Shawn, and all the children, to help me spread the joy of Christmas all year long.*

*Thank you, Kayla, for being such a caring girl.*

*Merry Christmas! I love you very much.*

*Santa Claus*

Santa sealed the envelope and went to see if the sleigh was ready.

"Are we ready to visit the boys and girls?"

"We sure are, Santa Claus!  It's going to be a perfect Christmas!"

"Marvelous work, everyone! I'm very proud of you!" cheered Santa. He pinned a shiny new medal on Willikers that read, "Every Day Is Christmas Day!" Then Santa said, "Please see to it that all of my helpers get their medals, too, and be certain Kayla gets my letter."

"I promise, Santa Claus!" said Willikers.

Santa climbed into his sleigh and said,
"Get lots of rest everyone…because tomorrow is Christmas Day.
And what a Christmas it will be!"

"Ho!  Ho!  Ho!  Merry Christmas!" called Santa Claus
as the reindeer flew into the night.

"Merry Christmas, Santa Claus!"
answered the tiny citizens of Santa's Village.

And Santa was off to deliver special gifts to all the children of the world.

It was very, *very* early on Christmas morning when Santa Claus returned home from his trip around the world.

"What a night, Willikers!" said Santa as he settled into his chair.

"What a year, Santa Claus!" said Willikers. He was tired, too.

"I hope all the children are happy today!" Santa said as he drifted off to sleep. "I hope everyone has a very merry Christmas."

The next day, Santa's letter was hand-delivered to Kayla.
She read it right away.

Kayla imagined all the places Santa had visited in the last year.
She felt wonderful just thinking of all the children he had helped.

"When I grow up I want to be
just like Santa Claus," Kayla said.

"Me, too," said Shawn and Vivian and David.

The children decided to spread the joy of Christmas all year long.
And they agreed that giving of yourself is the greatest gift of all.

**THE END**